CHATHAM-KENT PUBLIC LIBRARY

# FOLLOW THAT GARBAGE!
## A JOURNEY TO THE LANDFILL

KEEPING CITIES CLEAN

BY BRIDGET HEOS • ILLUSTRATED BY ALEX WESTGATE

**AMICUS ILLUSTRATED**
is published by Amicus
P.O. Box 1329, Mankato, MN 56002
www.amicuspublishing.us

**COPYRIGHT © 2017 AMICUS.**
International copyright reserved in all countries. No part of this book may
be reproduced in any form without written permission from the publisher.

Paperback edition printed by RiverStream Publishing in arrangement with Amicus.
ISBN 978-1-62243-355-1 (paperback)

**LIBRARY OF CONGRESS CATALOGING-IN-PUBLICATION DATA**
Names: Heos, Bridget, author. | Westgate, Alex, illustrator.
Title: Follow that garbage! : a journey to the landfill / by Bridget Heos ; illustrated by Alex Westgate.
Description: Mankato, Minnesota : Amicus, [2017] | Series: Keeping cities clean |
Audience: K to grade 3. | Includes index.
Identifiers: LCCN 2015040672 (print) | LCCN 2015042224 (ebook) |
ISBN 9781607539636 (library binding) | ISBN 9781681510811 (eBook)
Subjects: LCSH: Refuse and refuse disposal—Juvenile literature. | Fills (Earthwork)—
Juvenile literature. | Recycling (Waste, etc.)—Juvenile literature.
Classification: LCC TD792 .H46 2017 (print) | LCC TD792 (ebook) | DDC 363.72/8—dc23
LC record available at http://lccn.loc.gov/2015040672

**EDITOR:** Rebecca Glaser
**DESIGNER:** Kathleen Petelinsek

**PRINTED** in the United States of America at
Corporate Graphics in North Mankato, Minnesota.

HC 10 9 8 7 6 5 4 3 2 1
PB 10 9 8 7 6 5 4 3 2 1

### ABOUT THE AUTHOR
Bridget Heos lives in Kansas City with her husband and four children. She has written more than 80 books for children, including several about the Earth and the environment. Find out more about her at www.authorbridgetheos.com.

### ABOUT THE ILLUSTRATOR
Alex Westgate is an illustrator, designer, and artist from Toronto, Ontario, Canada. He has worked for *The Washington Post*, BBC, *Reader's Digest*, and more. He drinks tap water, recycles, and throws things in the garbage every day.

Every week, the garbage truck takes your trash. Have you ever wondered where it goes? Let's follow the bags and find out!

Bags from each house are thrown in the hopper. They are smashed and pushed to the big part of the truck.

Inside, a moving wall smashes the garbage.
That way, it takes up less space.

6

A garbage truck can hold about 7 tons (6.35 metric tons) of trash! And it's not the only truck collecting garbage. In a large city like New York, there are more than 2,000 garbage trucks on the job every day. They collect trash from apartments, schools, city trash cans, and more.

When the truck is full, it heads to the transfer station. Here, the trash waits for its ride to the landfill.

The truck backs up and dumps out the trash. Trash is everywhere! But it will only be here for a little while.

Look, there's a milk jug, a pop can, and some paper. They can be recycled. In some cities, workers at the transfer station send these items to recycling centers. But in other places, recyclables wind up at the landfill.

WHY ARE WE HERE?

HELLO!
WE'RE NOT TRASH.
WE CAN BE RECYCLED!

The trash continues on its journey. A front loader pushes it over a ledge.

A trash compactor is below. It squishes the garbage even more. Next, an arm pushes the smashed trash into a semitruck. It can carry 48,000 pounds (22,000 kg) of trash!

ARE WE THERE YET!?

DUMP

Road trip! Most landfills are far away from cities.
That way, the smell doesn't bother the people in town.

WHAT A DUMP!

Here it is: the landfill. It's a giant hole lined with plastic. The plastic seals in the trash so it doesn't pollute the ground.

16

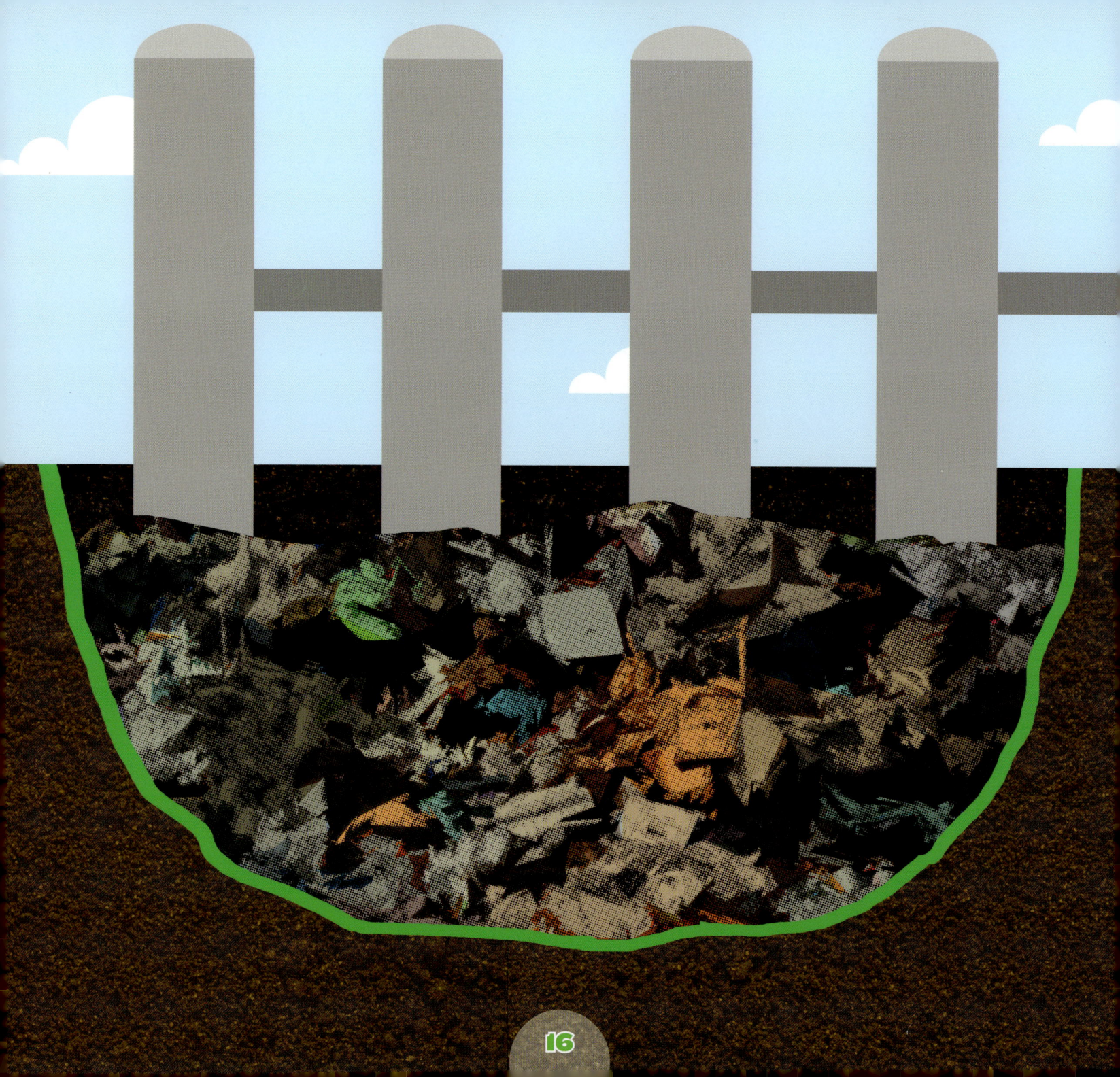

More trash comes in all day. In the evening, the trash is covered with dirt. That cuts down on the smell. The smell comes from a gas called methane. Some of the methane gas is captured and used to make energy.

More trash is added the next day. And the next. Finally, there is a hill of trash. Grass grows over it. Below, the trash rots away. But it could take 500 years or more.

Americans throw away about 250 million tons (226.8 metric tons) of garbage each year. It really adds up.

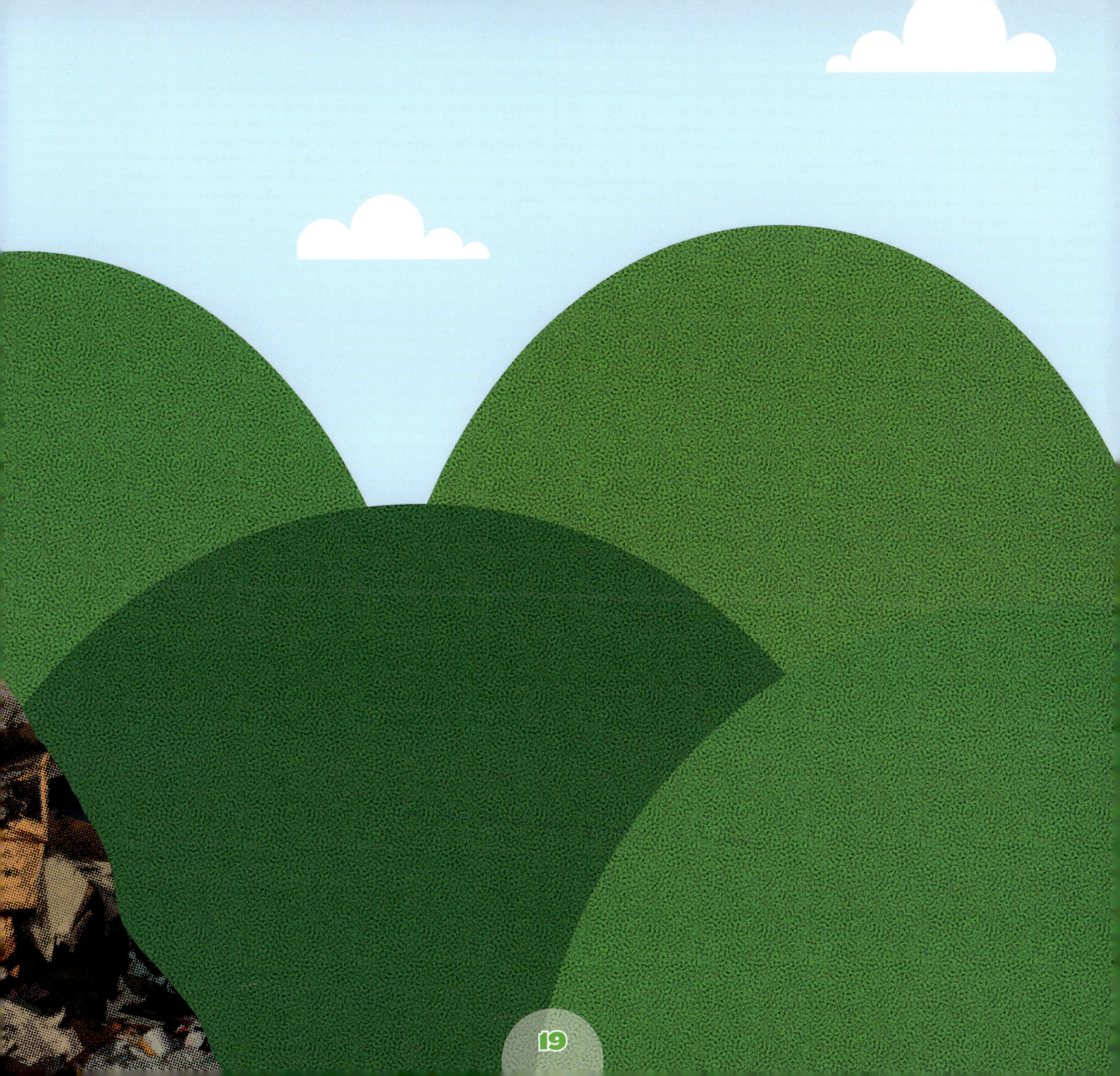

Not all trash goes to a landfill. Some is taken to a building where it is heated to 2700°F (1482°C), hotter than molten lava! Most of it turns into gas for energy.

WE USED TO BE TRASH LIKE YOU.

BUT NOW WE'RE HELPING BUILD A ROAD.

The leftovers are trapped in glassy sludge, which is broken up into rocks that can be used for roads. One man's trash is another man's treasure!

## RECYCLE IT YOURSELF
# MAKE SOIL FROM TRASH

Did you know you can turn trash from your kitchen, such as fruit and vegetable peels, into soil? This is called composting, and it's another way to recycle.

**What You Need:**

- [ ] Fruit and vegetable scraps
- [ ] Coffee grounds
- [ ] Grass clippings
- [ ] Eggshells
- [ ] Leaves, cardboard, or newspaper
- [ ] Shovel

## What You Do:

1. In a corner of your yard or an enclosed bin, create a compost pile.
2. Layer leaves, cardboard, or newspaper with grass clippings, fruit and vegetable scraps, coffee grounds, and eggshells.
3. Don't compost meat, oil, or dairy products, as this will attract pests.
4. Keep damp. Rainwater may be enough, but if the pile gets dry, add some water.
5. With a shovel, turn the pile every few days. If you don't turn it, it takes longer.
6. In about a month, you will have soil that you can use for a garden. The nutrients from the fruits, vegetables, and other trash will help new plants grow.

# GLOSSARY

**hopper** The container in a garbage truck where trash is stored.

**landfill** A place where trash is buried and stored underground for a long period of time.

**methane** Gas given off by rotting trash.

**recyclable** An item that can be broken down so that its materials can be made into something else.

**transfer station** A building where trash is stored until it can be transported to its final destination.

**trash compactor** A machine that smashes trash so that it takes up less space.

## READ MORE

Glaser, Linda. **Garbage Helps Our Garden Grow: A Compost Story**. Minneapolis: Millbrook Press, 2010.

Marsico, Katie. **Stinky Sanitation Inventions**. Minneapolis: Lerner, 2014.

Roza, Greg. **Landfills: Habitat Havoc**. New York: Gareth Stevens, 2014.

Tilmont, Amy. **Trash Talk: What You Throw Away**. North Mankato, Minn.: Norwood House Press, 2012.

## WEBSITES

**A Day in the Life of Your Garbage and Recyclables**
https://www.youtube.com/watch?v=TOpYa5OKGgY
Watch this video to see how garbage and recyclables are processed.

**EcoKids: Take Action**
https://ecokids.ca/take-action
The games and activities on this site teach you how to reduce the amount of garbage you throw away.

**Idaho PTV: Science Trek: Garbage**
http://idahoptv.org/sciencetrek/topics/garbage/index.cfm
Watch a video, play games, and learn all about what happens to our garbage after it gets picked up.

**National Institutes of Environmental Health Science: Kids' Pages**
http://kids.niehs.nih.gov/explore/reduce/
Learn about how you can reduce the amount of trash that winds up in landfills.

*Every effort has been made to ensure that these websites are appropriate for children. However, because of the nature of the Internet, it is impossible to guarantee that these sites will remain active indefinitely or that their contents will not be altered.*